Seeking Marlo

By Louis Rosenberg and Joe Rosenbaum

Art by Bill Maus

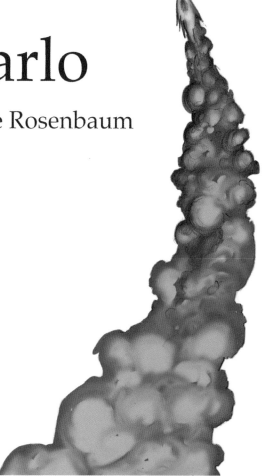

Outland Pictures

Billy was like any boy…

He loved building robots, shooting rockets, playing shortstop,
and sliding into home plate.

There was never a day he didn't come home covered in mud and grease, with twigs in his hair.
But these days, he didn't feel like doing much of anything...

"For the last time, Billy," his mother called out.
"Go outside—now!"

"Yeah… yeah… I'm going!" Billy moaned as he trudged outside.

He passed his bicycle. His skateboard. His remote control car, modified for jousting.

But there was nobody to joust with.

His best friend Marlo had moved away,
taking his own "super-joust-mobile" with him.

So Billy went to his special place…

A place that had once reached high up into the clouds…
But for some reason, the tree no longer seemed that tall.

The reason was Marlo.

Without him, nothing was very much fun.

The treehouse had once been their secret hideout.

Their clubhouse.   Their dugout.   Their command-station.   Their research lab.

But now it was just Billy's.

The treehouse was also the place where he and Marlo had repaired that old TV.

They had found it on the side of the road, tossed out with banana peels and soda cans.

They spent weeks getting the old thing to work, but then, they were too busy to ever watch it.

But now, it sure was useful…

"Are you coming swimming with us?" a voice rang from outside.
It was Billy's little sister, Lauren...

She knew she wasn't welcome near "Command Station 6" but her Mom had sent her anyway.

"No..." Billy yelled back, not bothering to get up.
"NO! NO! NO!"

Sinking deeper into his beanbag chair, Billy watched and watched and watched, when…
The old TV started flickering… and flashing… and then it suddenly went DEAD.

Billy tried and tried,
but he couldn't make the TV turn back on again!

"Oh, come on…" Billy snarled, but for some reason that didn't fix the problem.
So he pulled himself up with a sigh and a frown, and opened the back of the old TV.

As he slowly reached in - "OUCH!"

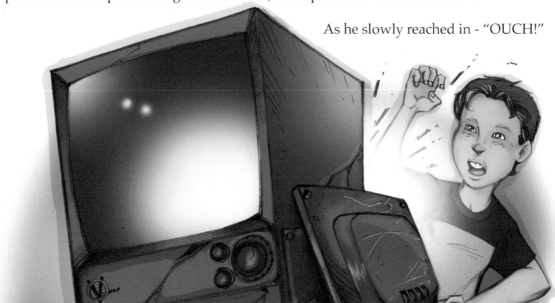

That's when Billy remembered the 'REPAIR GUIDE' left by Marlo.

Billy followed the steps, first yanking the plug, then reaching in...
Then he slowly pulled out an old, dusty, crusty, burnt-out fuse.

"Good call," he said. "Thanks, Marlo."

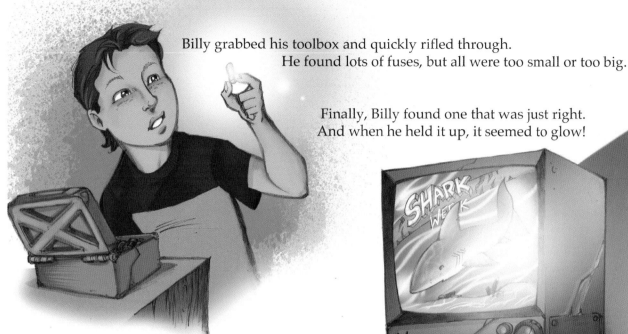

Billy grabbed his toolbox and quickly rifled through.
He found lots of fuses, but all were too small or too big.

Finally, Billy found one that was just right.
And when he held it up, it seemed to glow!

"What the--?" Billy gasped, but the glow faded away.
So he plugged the fuse into the TV and hit the remote.

The TV roared to life -- "The Tiger Shark may not be the largest
man-eater in the ocean, but it's the most agressive..."

What Billy didn't notice was that he hadn't plugged the TV
back into the electrical outlet!

There was something else that Billy didn't notice.

Billy hit the remote again, searching for cartoons. Instead, an ancient volcano erupted on the screen.

Click! Billy changed the channel and saw ants swarming over an ant hill.

There was a loud rumbling coming from outside the window.

Billy slowly turned, confused…

THUMP! THUMP! THUMP!

Billy ran over and looked outside. He couldn't believe his eyes!

Click! Click! Click!

Every time Billy changed the channel,
the world outside his window
changed, as well.

One second he was in the Arctic…
then in outer space…then in the midst
of an old battle.

MARLO

But he stopped clicking when he saw a dirt path
that wound through the hills. A large wooden sign pointed down the path.

"Marlo?" Billy said. "Marlo!"
Billy grabbed his sweatshirt and headed down the ladder.
But everything was different …the tree was now 100 feet tall!

When Billy finally reached the bottom, he started down the winding path,
eager to find Marlo. But around every turn, was another turn - it just stretched on and on...

Billy was growing discouraged, when he heard two boys laughing up ahead!

He took off running towards the sound...

Billy was disappointed.

He didn't recognize either of the boys.

Suddenly, one of the them got a bite. It nearly pulled the rod out of his hands. The other boy dropped his rod and grabbed his friend by the shoulders.

"Hey, kid," he called out to Billy. "We need some help! This one's huge!"

"I—I don't know how to fish…" Billy answered.

"I'm just looking for my friend, Marlo. I thought he might be here."

Suddenly the big fish yanked hard, and the boys nearly fell over.

"Come on, kid! Help us…
We need to pull!"

Behind him, a giant fish leapt from the tiny pond, but Billy didn't see it...
He was already back on the path looking for Marlo, and it wasn't going well.

Billy walked and walked and walked…

He almost gave up, but then…
he saw something that gave him hope.

Nobody loved candy as much as Marlo!

Then Billy heard the crack of a bat and kids cheering!

He rushed towards the sound and found...a baseball game, boys against girls.

Nobody loved baseball as much as Marlo!

"Come on, Stevie - give her the heat!" a fielder called out.

Stevie wound up and pitched a mean slider, but the girl at bat hit the ball squarely and made it to first base.

Billy looked around and saw a boy in the outfield chomping on a Snickers bar.
And he definitely wasn't Marlo.

"Yo, buddy," the pitcher called to Billy. "Can you play third? We're getting creamed out here."

"No… no thanks," Billy answered. "I think I got the wrong game."

"Come on, pal," the pitcher pleaded. Billy just shook his head.

Another girl had come up to bat, as tiny as could be. "Quit stalling," she yelled. "Let's play ball!"

Billy backed away and started down the path again.

He didn't even hear the crack of the bat…
Or see the ball, soaring high into the air, over the distant hills.

Billy continued on, walking and walking…
Until he saw something up ahead – SMOKE - like the plume
from a model rocket.

He ran towards it. After all… nobody liked rockets
more than Marlo!

Cresting the hill, Billy spotted a valley ahead, three kids getting ready to launch another rocket.

They were too far away to see their faces, but one of them could be Marlo.

So Billy ran down into the valley,
    nearly tripping on a log hidden in the grass…

"Marlo!" Billy called out, as he neared the kids – "Is that you?"
    They were crowded around the biggest model rocket he'd ever seen!

"Hurry up!" the girl in the lab coat barked. "The window's closing."

"I know," said the boy rolling out the wire – "I know!"

Billy watched, stunned, as the kids worked frantically...

The girl in the lab coat spotted Billy and held up a spare set of goggles.

"You better get these on," she yelled to him,
"we're launching in ten seconds."

"Wait!" Billy said. "Have you guys seen Marlo?"

"Who's Marlo?" the girl said.

"If you don't put on some goggles,
you better clear out."

Dejected, Billy turned and headed back towards the path...
As he walked away, the countdown began – 10, 9, 8...
But Billy was too sad about Marlo to hear the booming voice
of Mission Control:

"Houston, we have ignition... 3,2,1—and we have liftoff!"

Billy kept walking down the path, but he was
getting tired…

He had covered lots and lots of ground —
but no Marlo.

He was about to give up hope when he saw the sign up ahead.

It was the same sign he'd followed at the start of his quest,
with one major difference.

This time, the sign was pointing directly
at his treehouse.

Billy rushed up the ladder and into his treehouse,
expecting to find Marlo waiting for him.

But once again, he was disappointed.

This was too much. Billy wasn't sad anymore. He was mad.

"You lied to me!" Billy shouted at the smashed TV
through his tears.
"You said I'd find Marlo. You said...
but he's gone!"

That's when he saw something unexpected...

Billy reached into the mess of parts and pieces and pulled out the fuse.

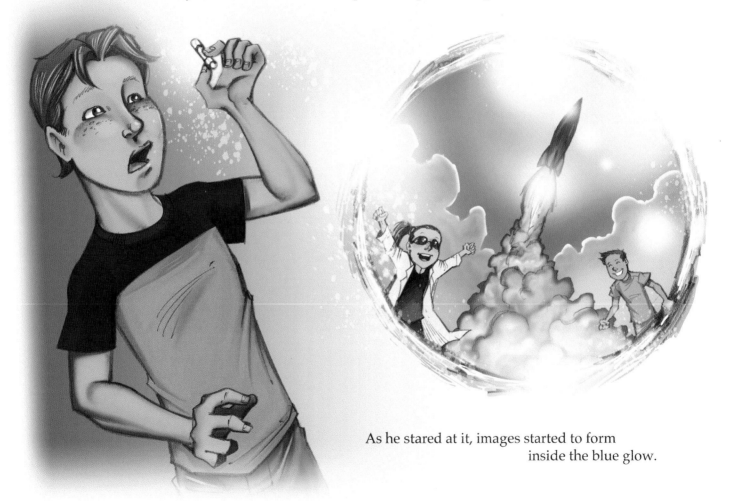

As he stared at it, images started to form
inside the blue glow.

The next day, Billy showed up at the beach club.
He hadn't been there in a very long time.

He walked out on the diving board, took a deep breath, and...

Bonk! A soccer ball bounced off Billy's head as he came up out of the water.
"Sorry, that's mine..." a boy named Scott called out.

Billy watched as Scott kicked the ball against the wall.
It hit and bounced away again. "You need some help?" Billy asked.
"Yeah, this wall's not much of a goalie," Scott said. "Do you play?"

"No," Billy said, climbing out of the pool. "But I could learn."

A streak in the sky made them both look up. It was a model rocket.

"That thing's gonna hit the moon," Scott laughed.
"Totally…" Billy agreed.

The years went by, and Billy found lots of new friends, like Scott.

But he would never forget Marlo.

Or any of his other friends.

www.outlandpictures.com

Printed in Poland
by Amazon Fulfillment
Poland Sp. z o.o., Wrocław

66384601R00023